THE GRIMSTONES

WHIRLWIND

by Asphyxia

the third magnificently
secret diary of
Martha Grimstone

ALLEN&UNWIN

SYDNEY • MELBOURNE • AUCKLAND • LONDON

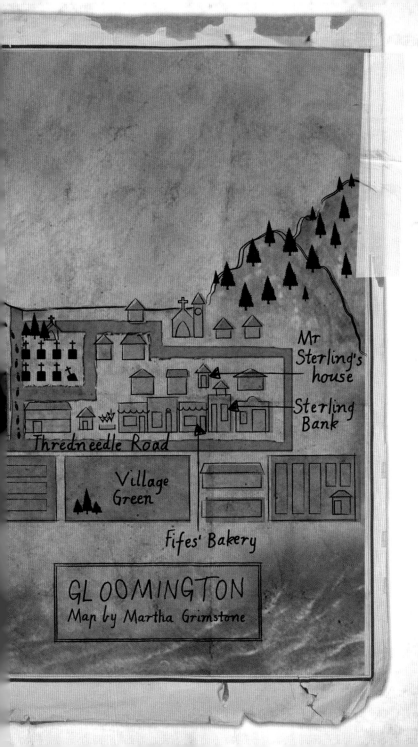

Mr
Sterling's
house

Sterling
Bank

Thredneedle Road

Village
Green

Fifes' Bakery

GLOOMINGTON
Map by Martha Grimstone

Allen & Unwin
83 Alexander Street
Crows Nest NSW 2065
Australia
Phone: (61 2) 8425 0100
Fax: (61 2) 9906 2218
Email: info@allenandunwin.com
Web: www.allenandunwin.com

A Cataloguing-in-Publication entry is available
from the National Library of Australia
www.trove.nla.gov.au

ISBN 978 1 74331 300 8

Cover and text design by Jenine Davidson
Cover photograph by Taras Mohamed
Set in 11 pt Bookman Old Style by Jenine Davidson
Internal photographs by Asphyxia,
Adis Hondo (www.handinhand.com.au) and
Taras Mohamed (www.tarasmohamed.com)
Artwork by Asphyxia and Jenine Davidson
This book was printed in September 2012 at
Everbest Printing Co Ltd in 334 Huanshi Road South,
Nansha, Guangdong, China.

1 3 5 7 9 10 8 6 4 2

THE

GRIMSTONES

Created & written
by Asphyxia

Designed and typeset by Jenine Davidson

Big Ideas, especially for story
and characters, by Paula Dowse
and Kelly Parry

Photographs by Adis Hondo,
Taras Mohamed and Asphyxia

Illustrations by Jenine Davidson
and Asphyxia

Fantastic editing by Eva Mills,
Elise Jones and Rosalind Price

Little ideas by Jesse Dowse

www.thegrimstones.com

SUNDAY

My Dearest Diary,

Something fateful and terrible happened today. I simply cannot believe it. I feel like a balloon with all the air let out. I am deflated and discombobulated both, as my Aunt Gertrude would say.

But pardon me – I'm getting ahead of myself. Let me explain from the start...

It happened this morning. We were in the kitchen, toasting mallowberries. Have you ever tasted a mallowberry? Since you are merely a book, I expect you haven't. They are the most exquisite thing. Delicately warmed, they are at once sweet and sour, and set your mouth on sparkle with little fizzing pops. But if you don't toast them it's like chewing a rubber sponge. Which is why I invented my Mallowberry Toasting Device:

'Crumpet, another twig, please, a big one,' I ordered, and my baby brother tossed me a small stick from the woodpile by the kitchen stove.

The Mallowberry Toasting Device was not performing well. The flame was too small, the berries weren't warm enough, and there was a growing pile of berry spit-outs on a plate on the kitchen table.

'That's enough, Martha Grimstone,' Aunt Gertrude said sternly. 'You'll burn the place down.' She turned back to the stove, where she was cooking something for Sunday lunch that would no doubt taste disgusting. Aunt Gertrude only ever cooks sensible things. Her idea of a feast is boiled brussels sprouts with three grains of salt, mashed turnips and rhubarb for dessert.

My mama, Velvetta Grimstone, swept into the kitchen to fetch a cup of tea. 'Drink it here, Mama,' I begged, patting the seat beside me. 'I'll toast you a mallowberry.' Not even Mama, who is normally far too busy sewing, can resist the lure of a mallow-berry. I nudged my chair closer to hers, checked Aunt Gertrude wasn't looking, and poked a small log into the fire rather than Crumpet's stick.

At least Mama never worries about the house burning down. All she can think about is whether to stitch a gossamer or velvet lining into Mrs Gold-ing's coat, and whether she's remembered to tell my dead father about Crumpet's latest antics. Yes, you read that correctly: my father *is* dead, and Mama still visits him in the crypt every single day, to talk to him.

Grandpa Grimstone entered the room, mut-tering to himself about salt. He spends his days in his apothecary, the most magnificent room in our home, concocting potions to heal everything from leg-boils to a broken heart. Actually, that's not true – he doesn't know how to cure a broken heart, or he would have fixed Mama's long ago. But he does heal the villagers of every ailment imaginable, and he tries his best to use magic to help ease the terrible storms that trouble our valley. The apothecary is filled with mysterious jars of herbs, devilsnake eyeballs and dust from the skeletons of extinct creatures, but every now and then Grandpa Grimstone needs something utterly ordinary, like salt.

He was rummaging in the pantry when the kitchen door creaked and our gardener, August, appeared. 'Excuse me, ma'am, there's a parcel,' he said to Aunt Gertrude, blushing a little. We all looked up expectantly.

'Come in, boy – is it the lyssidious rhyzomes?' Grandpa asked.

'That must be the velvet I ordered last month,' Mama said at the exact same moment.

August examined the sender's address. 'Err, no, I believe it's from Lady Sterling.'

A shimmer of excitement rippled through the kitchen. Even the mallow-fire flame leapt a little higher. Lady Sterling is the most glamorous person I have ever met. And the kindest. The most gracious.
I remembered her fingering my plaits and admiring our home when she'd come to our summer solstice party with her nasty son, Mr Sterling, who she was visiting from the city at the time.

We all gathered around eagerly as Aunt Gertrude snipped the string and unwrapped the paper.

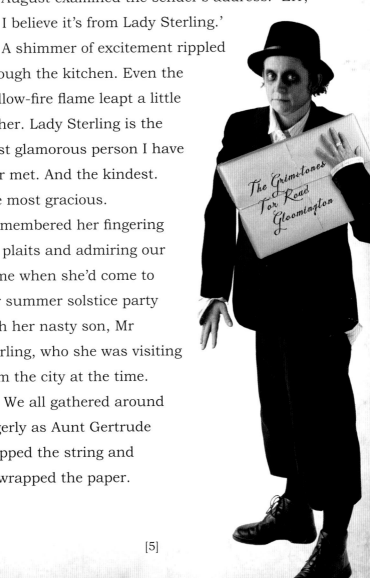

The Grimstones
Tor Road
Gloomington

My dear Grimstones,

I can't thank you enough for your gracious hospitality on the summer solstice. You are clearly a family of very talented individuals, and I write to ask if I might obtain your services.

Dear Velvetta, the suit you made for August was the best-crafted garment I have ever seen. May I order one just like it for my son, Furchell? I have enclosed fabric, also, for an evening gown for myself, of whichever design you feel would be most flattering. My measurements are attached.

Elcho, I have searched high and low for ficklepods in recent years, and was so excited to learn that they grow in your valley. If you've enough to spare, may I request a 3-ounce jar of them, please?

And Martha. Your musical aptitude has left me stunned. The Queen's Music Academy is just blocks from my home, and I cannot banish the thought that you must receive formal training to further your gift. I took the liberty of enquiring on your behalf, and told Madame Sonatine, the headmistress, all about you. They would be delighted to receive you, should you wish to pursue this. Tuition fees are covered by the state, and Martha, I would be most delighted to accommodate you at my home for the duration of your studies.

I shall be visiting my son on the 23rd of next month, and will call on you that afternoon, if this is agreeable to your family.

Yours in anticipation,

Lady Audraletta Sterling

The Queen's Music Academy

Here at the Queen's Music Academy we offer programs for all levels of study, from beginner to advanced. Age requirements are flexible.

The academy's diverse curriculum and its highly qualified faculty of professional artists/teachers ensure success in the pupil's chosen field. In addition to an established reputation as
faculty

Oh Diary, I fear I must have eaten a halluci-berry by mistake, for surely I could not have read correctly?

Yes! OH, YES YES

YES YES YES!

I have inherited my father's musical ability, and I finally managed to decode his cryptic worksheets recently … all except the one written on the day of his death. My father used his music to command the weather, and I have learned his secrets!

I can bring sunshine, breezes and rain, and send errant clouds scudding across the sky.

Sometimes, at least. It only seems to work when I'm in the right mood. And I can barely grasp at the edges of what my father was trying to do with his music when he died: he wanted to learn to calm a storm the way Grandpa can with his magic, but he died trying.

Oh, how I long to understand it all. And at music school they will help me find the answers, I am sure of it! I must, I SIMPLY MUST, go to the Queen's Music Academy! I shall live with Lady Sterling in her stately manor by the Saint Terese Gardens. It will probably have a rotunda and a lake – with a family of ducklings who will queue up to be fed the crumbs when we take scones with jam and cream there on a Sunday afternoon. Lady Sterling will invite all her elegant friends to come when I graduate dux of the school, wearing a gown made entirely of gossamer thread, sewn by Mama especially for the occasion. And I shall be Lady Martha the Magnificent Queen of Music, collecting my award for Extraordinary Musical Accomplishments, and playing a melody for the audience that will bring urchins to the windows and a tear to Lady Sterling's eye. Oh,

the splendour of it!

But Grandpa Grimstone said:

'Martha is far too young for that.'

'I think music school is a lovely idea,' Mama argued. 'But goodness, I think I should miss Martha too much if she were to leave us.'

'I don't wish to be unkind, Martha dear,' continued Grandpa, 'but I don't feel you are quite trustworthy enough yet to venture so far from home. There is an impetuousness about you that you need to learn to control.'

I wanted to race to the apothecary and find an agreeability spell to make Grandpa Grimstone say yes to every wonderful notion ever presented to him – or perhaps a spell of fancy, showing him all the magnificent possibilities that may await me if he says yes.

Instead, I took a deep breath and said politely, 'Grandpa, that's simply not true. I am perfectly trustworthy. I might have had my impetuous moments, but those days are well and truly behind us now, I can assure you.'

I was sure that had done the trick, but then Aunt Gertrude said, 'Martha cannot possibly abscond as Lady Sterling suggests. She is necessitated here. Who would tend to Crumpet in her absence? Who would fetch the daily milk and bread, and manage the quails? I certainly cannot be expected to take on any further responsibilities.'

There was silence, for I didn't know the answer to these questions. At the very thought of leaving Crumpet behind, my heart *WHOMPED* out of my chest and straight onto the floor. And I had to admit that offloading my boring daily chores on Aunt Gertrude could be seen as impetuous. Instead of responding, we all looked at Mama and August, who were both gazing dreamily at the fabric Lady Sterling had sent.

'This is the finest fabric I have ever seen,' Mama breathed, incredulity in her voice. 'I believe it's the arachnarina fabric I read about in Bobbin & Co's last catalogue, woven from the cobweb of the philistimist spider. I tried to order some, but they only had one piece and it had already been sold. It's just as well – it was frightfully expensive.'

'It would be perfect for a wedding dress,' August said, looking sidelong at Aunt Gertrude.

She ducked her head and shushed him. 'No one's proposed to me yet,' she said under her breath.

August works for us, doing his best to keep our rattly, big old house in good repair and the weeds away from Grandpa Grimstone's herbs. For as long as I can remember, he's been in love with Aunt Gertrude. Just recently, due to certain events on the summer solstice, Aunt Gertrude has been showing signs that the feeling could be mutual.

I was hoping August would get down on his knee right there and then ... but that never happened, because unfortunately there was a loud

 and

from the Mallowberry Toasting Device.

Nooooooo!

'Crumpet, Help!'

I cried.

Crumpet crawled to the table (and he crawls very fast, because he has three legs) and puffed delicately, extinguishing the flame.

The good thing about having a baby brother with a magical gift is that he can take care of house fires whenever they nearly occur. The bad thing is that not even Crumpet's magical gift was enough to save the fabric.

We all stared at
the charred remains.
Lady Sterling will
never want me to
board with her now.
I've ruined

EVERY-
THING!

'Martha, I don't
think your impetuous
days are quite
over yet,' Grandpa
Grimstone said.

SATURDAY

Today the market was hosted on our village green. This only happens once a year; the market is held in a different village each month.

We all had a bath and put on our best clothes. August tied Crumpet to my back and we set off down the hill, just like a proper family – Aunt Gertrude and Grandpa Grimstone in front, followed by Mama, with August, Crumpet and me trailing behind.

Usually I'd have been fit to burst with the excitement of it all. I'd have had a nice rhythm going, scraping my boots against the stone, giving little skippety-kicks and humming to create a melody. The bird who follows me everywhere would have perched on my shoulder and joined in with vigorous cheeps.

Today, though, all I could think of was Lady Sterling's ruined fabric, and missing my chance to go to music school, and how I might never learn to control my musical gift now. I had thought of nothing else all week long. I hummed a doleful tune and plonked my feet down. A cold breeze nipped around my ankles, and a miserable rain cloud in the shape of a weeping willow hovered above my head. My bird flew alongside me, squawking in protest, and Crumpet whined and squirmed on my back.

I kicked out hard at a boulder beside the path, and pain shot up my leg.

'Sloff,' said Crumpet, patting my cheek with his chubby little hand. Immediately the pain subsided, and I blew him a thank-you kiss.

Things got even worse, though, because a few minutes later we walked smack into a whirlwind. It was just big enough to wrap around Crumpet and me, its tentacles reaching inwards devilishly to pluck at my dress and snatch at my plaits.

Grandpa Grimstone frowned heavily. 'A storm is coming,' he announced. 'We must hurry at the market, for we may not have much time.'

Our valley is plagued by the most terrible storms, which uproot our precious herbs, smash our windows, and bring all sorts of trouble to everyone who lives here. Grandpa Grimstone works hard to cast magic so that the eye of the storm passes some distance away in the woods, but it's very difficult and he doesn't always succeed.

The whirlwind coiled closer, whispering against my leg and slithering upwards until it had grasped me firmly around the waist. I fanned out my fingers, and a sense of foreboding tingled in my fingertips and slowly spread through my whole body. The whirlwind was like the toe of the storm – dipping itself into our valley before the storm burst upon us, howling and screaming. At least a whirlwind gave us warning that we had to prepare ourselves, but I wished I could just STEP on it and—

STEP ON IT?

I had an idea! If the whirlwind were the toe of the storm, and you were to squish it, would this mean that the storm would no longer advance? The cogs in my mind sped up so much that I was sure steam was about to whistle out of my ears like a kettle come to boil. For surely I can find some way to cast musical notes to stop a whirlwind? Stomp on that toe? Dispel it before it can turn into a storm?

I realised right then that if I can't go to music school to learn how to use my special talent, well

Dear Diary, I am just going to have to teach myself! Even though I have absolutely no idea where to start...

The wind curled itself around my neck, raising goosebumps, and on my back Crumpet squirmed again. I realised the rest of my family had gone ahead, and hurried to free myself of the whirlwind's grasp. 'Sorry,' I said to Crumpet. But in my mind all I could think was, *There must be a way, there must. And I will find it!*

The market was busy, bustling with people from every village in our valley. I spied a gypsy wagon I'd never seen before, its side uncovered to reveal trinkets, fabric, jewels and many unidentifiable odds and ends. August was talking to the pedlar when I approached, gesturing to a pretty silver ring set with a large ruby. He'd emptied his money-jar into his palm and was holding out his pitiful stash.

Poor August. He doesn't have any savings, as he's always using his money to buy things we need for household repairs. And most Mondays, when Aunt Gertrude is supposed to pay him, he ends up saying, 'There now, I'm fine, you give it to me next week.'

'I'm sorry,' the pedlar said to August. 'The ring is worth at least five times that.'

August sighed. 'Maybe next time,' he mumbled. And to me: 'I'd best help your Aunt Gertrude with the flour.' He ambled away, his shoulders drooping.

I soon forgot August's troubles, though, because hanging from the wagon railing was an ornate cage holding two of the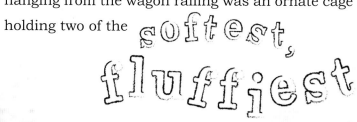

white creatures I'd ever seen. I held out my fingers and one of them sniffled at me, its little black velvety nose rubbing my fingernail. My heart sprouted rose petals of love that melted into big fat drips, right down into my stomach.

'What are they?' I asked the pedlar.

'Rabbits. Angora rabbits. That's why they're so fluffy.'

I looked again and saw long bunny ears hiding in the puffs of fur. He was right!

The other rabbit, this one with a pink nose, also nuzzled my fingertips. My stomach gurgled with the warm, bubbly feeling of falling in love. I could imagine myself as mama to these two exquisite creatures, who would follow me around day and night, sleep curled at my feet, and stare at me all day with wide eyes of devotion, as they were doing right now. I *had* to take them home with me.

'Where did they come from?' I asked the pedlar, as an excuse to stay. I hadn't a single coin to call my own.

'From the Pommington family, in yonder village.' The pedlar gestured vaguely behind him. 'A most unusual family. The mother, Agnetha Pommington –

do you know her? – she made herself a cup of tea with bark from the casselwyn tree, to cure her indigestion. But even *I* know it's the leaves that hold the cure, not the bark, silly woman. So of course next morning Mrs Pommington wakes up with amnesia – she's forgotten everything. In fact, she thinks she's the queen! Expects to be served day and night, waited on by her husband and children. Even demands her husband build her a throne to sit on! Poor Alfred and the children are going mad, what with looking after her and having to do all the cooking, washing, gardening and shopping themselves. That's why the rabbits had to go. Too much work. The others have all sold. These are the last two left.'

I reached inside the cage and sank my hand into the fur of the black-nosed bunny, rubbing his neck. It was like massaging a warm cloud. Crumpet stretched over my shoulder towards the cage, too, grasping the ironwork in his fingers and making little cooing noises.

'What they really need is memsparkym – the cure to her malady. Only they haven't a clue where to get any. I did have some once,' continued the pedlar, 'only I sold it to a family whose father had taken to sleeping in a kennel. I haven't seen any since.' He frowned and shook his head.

I, however, had seen memsparkym very recently. It grows on a vine creeping up the back of my father's crypt. I swallowed the excitement bubbling inside me like strawberry fizz-pop and eyed the pedlar levelly. 'Shall I do you a deal, sir? Memsparkym for these rabbits here?'

His eyes widened. 'You've got *memsparkym*?!'

I nodded, casual as I could manage, trying not to look at the rabbits. 'I certainly do. Shall we trade?'

'One flower per rabbit, and an extra one for the cage.'

'How about four flowers, and you include the ring in the deal?' I indicated the ring August had been admiring. A couple of fine droplets of rain landed on my cheek. Oh no, was the storm coming sooner than we'd thought?

'Nonsense, girl. That ring is worth a hundred memsparkym flowers.'

I sighed. There was no way the vine had a hundred flowers on it. I untied Crumpet and set him down beside the rabbit cage. 'You stay here,' I whispered, 'and don't let anyone else buy those rabbits.'

I ran like I'd never run before, through the drizzle, until I reached home. I fetched the ladder from the potting shed, and climbed up to pluck the flowers. At the top of the ladder I froze, remembering memsparkym flowers can't bear to get wet once they are plucked. I could have sent the rain clouds on their way by playing my father's wonderful invention, the Epithium (for thankfully they appeared to be normal clouds after all, not the storm come early) – but that takes time and focus, and I was simmering with excitement and impatience. Instead I dashed back to the potting shed and grabbed one of Grandpa Grimstone's plant-sized umbrellas. It was just big enough for the three memsparkym flowers, and I managed to get back to the market without a single drop of rain touching their petals.

The pedlar's eyes widened when he saw me. 'Good lord, girl! I thought you was telling me a falsehood. You really *do* have memsparkym!' He took the flowers from me eagerly and tucked them safely under his canvas, out of reach of the rain.

Then he handed me the rabbit cage, and they were mine,

mine,

MINE !!!

SUNDAY

I've named the rabbits. The pink-nosed one, the girl, is called Tillipilli, named for a plant that has fluffy white bolls on it just like a cotton plant does. And the boy with the velvety black nose I have called Ziphwort. The ziphwort is a white flowering herb with tiny black dots on it used to thaw the hardest of hearts – very fitting for a white rabbit with a black-dot nose.

However, sleeping with the rabbits curled around my feet last night did not go so well. At first they were happy to cuddle my toes, and I wriggled my feet to give them a little massage. But every time I nodded off my feet stopped massaging, and Tillipilli gave my littlest toe a nibble to remind me to get back to it. I tried setting them both on the floor but that was no good, either, for they hopped over to the antique chest of drawers that once belonged to my great-great-great-great-great (something like that) grandmother and started gnawing on the legs. Then they found one of my boots and chewed right through the laces. So I put them back in their little cage in the corner, where they finally curled up together and went to sleep.

Tillipilli and Ziphwort love their ornate cage, but it's far too small for them to stay in all day long. By mid-morning there were rabbit-sized bites all over the landing as well as my bedroom, and I realised they need their own quarters. So Crumpet and I are building them a castle, with a little help from the bird.

While I hammered together the joists for the roof, Crumpet held a fistful of pepperweed greens high above his head. 'Aklfft,' he said, and Ziphwort stood on his hind legs to nibble delicately at the leaves.

I clapped, and Ziphwort lowered his head in a graceful bow.

Crumpet gurgled with delight. Once he has them trained we can join the circus with our Furry Flying Fluff Ball Rabbit Act! (If I can't go to music school, the least I can do is join the circus. Even though I can't stop wondering about that whirlwind music...)

The Rabbit Hutch

Designed and (to be) built by Martha Grimstone

rainwater tank to collect fresh drinking water

hay storage (hay used for sleeping and eating)

food storage for pellets

double arched doors (must be rabbit-proof)

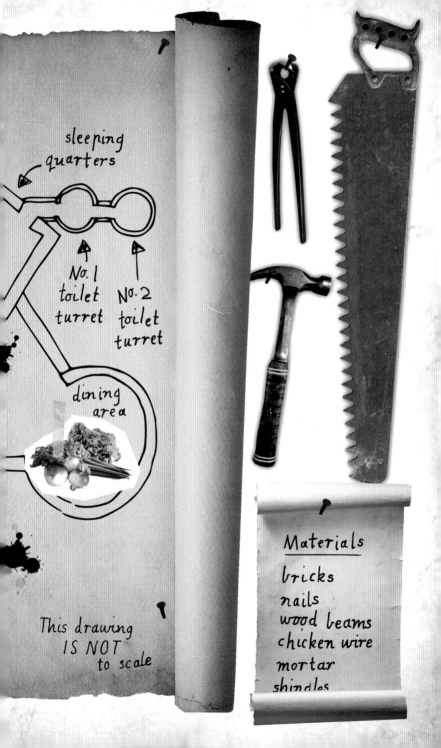

sleeping
quarters

Nº. 1
toilet
turret

Nº. 2
toilet
turret

dining
area

This drawing
IS NOT
to scale

Materials

bricks
nails
wood beams
chicken wire
mortar
shingles

'Aklfft,' Crumpet said again, holding the leaves above Tillipilli. But Tillipilli snorted rudely and turned away. Ziphwort rose again and bit off a mouthful of leaves, but instead of chewing them he offered them sweetly to Tillipilli. She nibbled contentedly.

'Oh, Tillipilli, surely you don't want Ziphwort to be the only star of the circus?' I asked her, stroking her ears, but she just eyed me warily, so I guess she's not really a Magnificent Circus Rabbit at heart. That's okay, though – I'm sure we'll find her own special talent soon.

'Plph,' said Crumpet, which meant it was six o'clock and I was to carry him to the kitchen for his nightly bottle of milky boilberry tea, and then tuck him straight into bed and sing him to sleep.

'Soon,' I promised. 'I'll just get the roof on the sleeping tower.' In a burst of cleverness earlier, I'd decided to build the roof on the ground and lift the whole thing, ready-made, onto the walls. I eased my fingers under the frame and tried to lift it ... but all it did was squash my fingertips – it was far too heavy. Now my idea didn't seem quite so clever.

'Pleeeeeeeph!' wailed Crumpet.

I sighed, realising I'd have to un-nail the middle bit and raise half the roof at a time. I cast around for the pincers.

Crumpet crawled to me and pummelled my legs with his tiny balled-up fists. 'Pleeeeeeeeeeeeph!!'

'Shhh, little one,' I said as soothingly as I could, while fighting a rising sense of panic. Where were the pincers? The storm hadn't arrived yet, but the clouds were thick and dark overhead, and night was falling fast.

Crumpet's red face had scrunched up like a dried trollberry. Fat tears squirted from his eyes alarmingly, splashing off the wall of the rabbit castle and *plink*ing into their water bowl. Crumpet is truly the sweetest brother imaginable, but miss the six o'clock deadline and everything changes. For once, just for *once*, couldn't he have some patience and wait for me to finish? His wail stretched around my head like Grandpa Grimstone's Storm Detector siren in a storm.

'ALL RIGHT! No roof for the castle tonight! The rabbits can stay in their TINY cage then!'

Crumpet cried harder at my outburst. He crawled to me and fastened his three legs around mine, his arms up, begging me to lift him; to make it good between us again.

I softened. 'Hold on, Crumpet, *please* hold on. I've got to put the rabbits back in their cage.' But of course he *was* holding on, and I couldn't walk at all. I tried an awkward jump, with Crumpet attached, but then he screamed blue murder.

I wished *I* could be the baby. I wanted to lie down and scream at everyone, and I wanted to finish the rabbit cage, which was so nearly there. And I DID NOT want to be interrupted to go and feed my little brother a bottle of milky boilberry tea.

Dear Diary, I eventually managed to get the rabbits into their cage, but by the time I'd carried both them and Crumpet to the house my eardrums were long burst, as was my patience. Aunt Gertrude had to help me hold Crumpet so I could feed him his tea, more of which ended up on the kitchen floor than in his belly, and then she had to call Grandpa Grimstone to help us carry Crumpet upstairs. Grandpa had been working nonstop since yesterday afternoon mixing potions and calling incantations to the sky, hoping he could hold the coming storm at bay. He emerged wearily from the apothecary, wiping his hands on his trousers, but even his stern presence couldn't settle Crumpet.

The three of us hauled Crumpet upstairs, his tiny limbs flailing angrily. I opened my mouth to begin his nightly lullaby, but there was no way I could be heard over his screams.

'Fetch the Epithium,' ordered Grandpa Grimstone.

There is one sound that soothes Crumpet most of all, and that's the patter of rain.

'But if I bring rain now, won't that risk bringing the storm, too?' I shouted over Crumpet's noise.

Grandpa Grimstone shook his head. 'The storm has a violent heart, which stirs up the rain clouds. But the rain clouds themselves are perfectly harmless. And besides, I fear this storm will come no matter what we do.'

I wheeled the Epithium into the bedroom and took a deep breath. Forcing myself to calm my thoughts, which were scuttling like ants in every direction, I ran my fingers over the strings. The notes rang out bold and clear, commanding. Crumpet's cries softened a little.

The music swept over all of us, cradling us, lifting us high, out of reach of tears and misery. Grandpa Grimstone and Aunt Gertrude tiptoed from the room and I played on, the melody loosening the tension in my shoulders. It took half an hour for the accompaniment to come – the first spatter of raindrops on the roof. And Crumpet finally fell asleep to the *patter-patter* of rain riding the notes of the Epithium.

MONDAY

At last the storm blew in, despite Grandpa's fervent work, just as he had predicted. It was dawn, and we gathered in the parlour for safety. I settled Crumpet, still asleep, onto a cushion by the fire, the rabbit cage next to him. Ziphwort and Tillipilli merely rubbed their faces with their paws before curling back into a fluffy ball of sleep. They were so sweet, but I still felt as gloomy as the shadows cast by the storm. The lines on Grandpa's face sagged more than usual, and I wished I'd been able to

stomp on that whirlwind with my music, to save him his endless toil.

'Martha, fetch Velvetta,' Aunt Gertrude ordered as soon as Crumpet was settled. I sighed.

Mama had spent the night in the crypt, as she sometimes does – or perhaps she'd stayed overnight at her sewing machine and had popped in to say good morning to my father before she took herself off to bed. Either way, I found her in the crypt wearing Mortimer's cloak, chattering animatedly to him.

'…and of course I checked all the fabric at the market, but there was nothing even faintly like the arachnarina fabric Lady Sterling sent us. Mortimer, I've no idea what we'll do. But Martha and Crumpet came home with a pair of Angora rabbits, who are awfully swee—'

'Mama!' I interrupted urgently.
'The storm is here.'
'Already?' She seemed surprised.
'It's taken days, Mama!' I hung my father's cloak back on its hook and hurried her to the parlour.

'Come sit on my knee, Martha,' Mama said once we'd arrived. 'I'll tell you about the rabbits we had when I was a little girl.'

I stared at her in surprise, my gloom forgotten in an instant. She'd had rabbits? I settled myself in her lap, my cheek against her heart, breathing in the scent of roses and thornbells Mama always carries with her.

'When I was a small child I lived with my grandmother, who was a weaver. A prodigious weaver. She made cloth finer than anything money could buy. To supply her with yarn, my mother spun. From the age of two she could turn a spindle, and by the time she was three years old her yarn was as fine and smooth as any maiden's. As my mother grew she learned to sew, too, until it was she who turned my grandmother's fabrics into first-class tailored garments. Much later, she taught me to sew... But I digress. My mother and grandmother kept rabbits – Angora rabbits.'

'Were they cute and fluffy, like Tillipilli and Ziphwort?'

'They were indeed. All Angora rabbits are fluffy, Martha. And our rabbits produced fur – great fluffy handfuls of fur – that my mother spun into the softest, warmest yarn. For Angora rabbit fur is seven times warmer than wool, and has not the slightest itch to it.'

I sat bolt upright. 'You mean you can spin their fur? And use it to make a fabric?!'

'Of course! That's what Angora rabbits were bred for. You snip off their fur with scissors, spin it and weave it. And the fabric is the softest, cosiest cloth you can imagine.'

'As lovely as Lady Sterling's fabric? The arachnarina kind?'

Velvetta nodded. 'Pure Angora fabric would be as lovely as that, yes. Usually spinners mix Angora with another fibre, to make their fabric stronger. It's Angora that makes it soft and warm. I've never seen a pure Angora fabric in the catalogue.'

Dear Diary, you know what I am thinking, don't you?

A plan is hatching, larger and more glorious than I could possibly have imagined. I KNOW HOW TO REPLACE LADY STERLING'S FABRIC! I shall spin and weave the fur from my very own Tillipilli and Ziphwort! AND ALL WILL BE SAVED! Lady Sterling will forgive me after all. I shall prove to Grandpa Grimstone that I am now a responsible, trustworthy person.

I SHALL WEAVE MY WAY INTO THE QUEEN'S MUSIC ACADEMY!!

'Mama, you will teach me to spin and weave, won't you?' I begged.

But Mama sighed. 'I can show you how to spin, though my yarn was never as smooth as my mother's. But I don't know how to weave – that's the tragedy.'

I stared at her, perplexed. 'But you grew up in the same house as your grandmother, watching her weave.'

'I did, sweetheart. But my mother kept me very busy spinning and sewing. I wanted to learn to weave, for I longed more than anything to create my very own garment, from the beginning. I wanted to feed the rabbits, cut their fur, spin it, weave it,

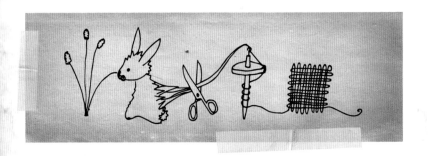

and then stitch it, all by myself. Fabric created at no cost – as the weeds the rabbits ate grew wild in our garden. It seemed like magic to me. So my grandmother promised that for my twelfth birthday gift she would teach me to weave. But Martha, a tragedy happened. We woke on the morning of my twelfth birthday and my grandmother had vanished.'

'Vanished? What happened to her?'

Mama's eyes glistened with unshed tears. 'I don't know. We never knew. She was just…gone.'

'Gone?! But surely after all these years you must know what happened to her?' I stared at Mama in disbelief.

'It remains a mystery. And so does weaving, to me. I never did learn.' Mama dabbed her eyes with a delicate lace handkerchief. 'The rabbits had to go, since we no longer had any use for their fur. We gave them to the Pommingtons, over yonder. And since then, I've had to make do with catalogue fabrics for my garments. They simply aren't the same.'

Poor Mama – she's known so much sorrow in her life. I wrapped my arms around her and buried my face in her neck. Perhaps *I* can work out the secret to weaving…and share it with Mama.

TUESDAY

Oh, help. Help help help. Dear Diary, whatever am I going to do NOW?!

Hold on, let me explain.

After hearing Mama's story yesterday, I made a decision: I shall put all my whirlwind-squishing aspirations out of my head – for now – and focus on the rabbits instead. I shall learn to use their fur to make fabric.

The storm passed without causing any great damage this time (phew), and August is setting the garden to rights today: massaging the spinifilus plant to straighten its stem; meticulously fetching back the bog-bean pods scattered far and wide throughout the garden. But first, yesterday after-noon, he helped me to hoist the roof onto the rabbit castle.

Ziphwort and Tillipilli spent their very first night in their new home last night, and when I checked in on them this morning after I'd fed the quails they hopped over to me for a cuddle and snuffled me with their faces as if to tell me how much they adored their new fortress.

So this afternoon, as soon as my chores and studies were out of the way, I grabbed Crumpet and a pair of Mama's sharpest scissors and we headed down to the castle to make our very first fur harvest. Mama told me the rabbits don't mind at all, so long as you leave them an inch of fur to keep them warm. It grows back again very quickly.

But as we rounded the mulberry tree and came into view of the castle, I could see immediately that something was wrong. **Very wrong.** **VERY VERY WRONG.** There was a large mound of dirt in the middle of the castle courtyard. And there was a new medieval feature that was most fitting to a castle, but not at all fitting to a rabbit cage: an earthen escape tunnel.

Worst of all:

there were

NO
RABBITS.

My mouth dropped open. My little babies had run away? Tears sprung to my eyes. What was wrong with the beautiful castle I'd built them? Why hadn't they wanted to stay? I stared at Crumpet in horror.

'Ork,' he said. He thinks they will come home tonight, when it grows dark.

I can only cross my fingers that he is right.

Rabbits rabbits

WEDNESDAY - EARLY MORNING

Diary, oh Dear Diary, the rabbits *didn't* return last night! What will I do? I'm so afraid I might never see my beautiful, floppy-eared darlings again. Just last week I felt perfectly whole, without having met the rabbits. But in the past few days I've fallen so very much in love that their absence leaves me empty and cold. Ziphwort? Tillipilli? Where are you?

WEDNESDAY - A BIT LATER

I'm writing this at the kitchen table, sneaking a few words here and there when Aunt Gertrude isn't looking. It's our daily education session, and Aunt Gertrude is determined I shall learn some advanced mathematics this morning.

'What's your knowledge of exponential growth, Martha?' she asked the second I sat down.

I shook my head and strummed my fingers on the table, humming the harried melody running through my mind:

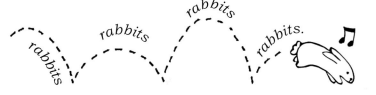

Aunt Gertrude rubbed her eyes, which had dark shadows beneath them. 'Shh. Please focus. We could employ exponential growth to improve the family's fiscal arrangements. Yes?'

I stared at her blankly. I hadn't the foggiest idea what she was talking about.

Aunt Gertrude sighed. 'I'm sorry, Martha. My explanation of this matter falls short. I'll reignite my mental faculties with a cup of tea, and re-attempt my elucidation after that.'

By which she meant she'll wake herself up with some tea and try again. Honestly, she needs a personal translator.

There is a custom in our valley for courting couples to take an evening walk together, once their chores are completed. And I have seen Aunt Gertrude and August slipping off together into the dark. But while most of the starry-eyed villagers are ready for their rendezvous by eight o'clock, poor Aunt Gertrude is rarely done before the small hours. It's Grandpa Grimstone's doing. We can never eat dinner until he's finished the day's potion-brewing, which means we usually sit down at the long and dusty dining table only shortly before midnight.

By the time we've eaten, and Aunt Gertrude has finished in the kitchen, it's one in the morning, or even later. And *then* she heads out with August. No wonder the food has been particularly brick-like recently and Aunt Gertrude is so hazy-minded she doesn't even realise I'm writing my diary right through our maths lesson...

Aunt Gertrude eventually returned, sipped her tea, and shook her head to clear it. 'All right. Suppose we were to ask one of Velvetta's customers to tell two new people about her work. If each of those two people were to make an order, and then tell two more people, who each did the same and so on, we would have an example of exponential growth for Velvetta's business. First we would receive two new orders, then four; the next week eight, the week after that sixteen, and the next week, thirty-two! That's exponential growth, Martha. It's an excellent technique to apply in business.'

I get it, I really do! In fact, I know that's *exactly* what will happen once I start making my beautiful Angora fabric! The exponential growth in demand will mean I'll have to work night and day, like my mama, to produce enough fabric. But unlike Mama,

I shall employ a whole team of people to assist – and build an entire rabbit *city* for all the rabbits that will be needed.

Well... I suppose that will only happen if I ever find my rabbits. I *will* find them, I *know* I will.

'Aunt Gertrude, do you think that as part of my education I could study textiles? For example spinning, and weaving?'

Aunt Gertrude stared at me in astonishment – probably because I'm always arguing against learning the domestic skills she wants to teach me. If she were properly awake she'd have stared me down and grilled me sternly on the fine points of exponential growth before allowing such a distraction. But today she rubbed her eyes again and said simply, 'That sounds like a marvellous idea, Martha. I shall seek out some books on the topic forthwith.'

Victory! This is the *very first* time I've ever had a say in my education! And as the topics foisted upon me by Aunt Gertrude are usually so boring, this is very exciting news indeed! It's—

OH*!*

I've forgotten what I was going to write, because guess who I have just seen? Ziphwort! Behind Aunt Gertrude. I'm trying not to look at him, so that she won't realise he's there and accuse me of irresponsibly losing my rabbits.

Oh dear. How on earth will I catch him without her noticing?!

WEDNESDAY…LATER STILL

'Martha,' Aunt Gertrude said eventually, 'this is regretful, but I simply must go and lie down. You are to prepare an example of exponential growth and present it to me tomorrow.'

As soon as she left I raced over to the fruit bowl – but Ziphwort took off at top speed. Who would have thought a fluff ball could move so fast? He hopped straight into the flour sack, which was sitting open on the kitchen floor. Just as I reached in to pluck him out, he burst out of the bag in a puff of flour and made for the other side of the kitchen. To my dismay, I realised there was now a nibble-sized hole in the sack, and that flour was spilling everywhere. I dusted it out of my eyes and turned after him.

'Here, Ziphwort, come here! I'll take you home.'

Instead of obeying, Ziphwort scampered across the kitchen bench, straight through the basket of quail eggs. I dived for it but was too late: the eggs rolled to the floor and smashed into a slippery, yolky mess. I skidded through the slime and almost grabbed him by the fur, but he slipped free and made a run for the pantry.

I slammed the pantry door shut behind him and stood there panting, my heart pounding, yolk squirming between my toes, flour puffing from my eyebrows.

I had imagined the rabbits would be like sweet

little children, obedient and loving. But it's dawning on me that Tillipilli and Ziphwort could be something else altogether…

I heard a strange sound from inside the pantry: Ping! Ping! Ping! I opened the door just a crack, blocking it with my foot to avoid any further escapes, and peered into the gloom. Ziphwort was sitting on the top shelf, licking his paws between nibbles as he ate his way through a bag of sultanas. He'd already attacked the sack of beans beside him, which now had a hole in it. The leftover beans were rolling out one by one, and each time one dropped I heard the noise again – PING! – as the bean hit the apple cider bottle below.

And here's the worst bit: even as I knew that I'd have to spend the entire afternoon cleaning up, and that Aunt Gertrude would yell at me for days over all the wasted food, my heart melted, because little Ziphwort was the sweetest thing on earth. He rubbed his furry paw behind his ears and stared at me contentedly.

I closed the pantry door and ran to fetch Crumpet. With his magical touch, I *knew* he'd be able to help me catch Ziphwort.

Crumpet was in the apothecary, working with a pendulum to slow the flow of sand through an hourglass.

I tell you, this is one of the UNFAIREST things about my life. While I endure hours of Aunt

Gertrude's tedium at the kitchen table, Crumpet studies with Grandpa Grimstone, learning the secrets of the apothecary. Grandpa Grimstone declares that Crumpet has a magical gift, while I do not. He once made the mistake of trying to teach his magical skills to someone who didn't have the gift, and it went very, very badly. So now he refuses to teach me. But Grandpa is *wrong*. I *do* have a magical gift, obviously. Look at the magic I used to make my own baby brother! Still, no matter how I argue, Grandpa Grimstone flatly refuses to see it my way, and I am banned from his apothecary's murky magnificence.

Thankfully Grandpa Grimstone was nowhere to be seen, so I hissed, 'Quick! Crumpet, I need your help. It's Ziphwort.'

He gurgled loudly (his way of laughing) and held his arms up to me. I scooped him up and hurried to the kitchen, fetching the ornate cage on the way. I placed the cage on the floor by the pantry door, smiled at Crumpet, and opened the door just a crack.

'Zttlip,' said Crumpet, and Ziphwort ate a last sultana before hopping gracefully down and curling up on Crumpet's lap as if it was his very own idea.

'Now to trim his fur.' I held up Mama's scissors.

Crumpet and Ziphwort eyed me uncertainly.

'Let's do it in the pantry,' I suggested, thinking that if Ziphwort were to make a run for it at least he wouldn't get far.

So we shuffled in and cleared a space amongst the beans and flour. I settled Ziphwort onto my lap, rubbing his favourite spot just under his ears. Then I grasped a handful of fur and made a quick snip, taking care to leave enough behind for Ziphwort, just as Mama had instructed. The fur came away freely, but Ziphwort got a terrible fright, snapping his head round and clanging his teeth on the scissors. I snatched my hands away, horrified, and Ziphwort took the opportunity to scuttle under the pantry shelves. He glared at me, his teeth chattering, his body coiled into a tense knot.

'Oh Ziphwort, I didn't mean to frighten you. Don't you want to help me make a new fabric for Lady Sterling?' I coaxed. 'Come on. This won't hurt – I'll leave plenty of fur for you, of course I will.'

'Krgg,' Crumpet whispered and Ziphwort

hopped towards him somewhat uncertainly. 'Krgg, krgg.' Ziphwort stretched out on the floor beside Crumpet.

Crumpet pointed to the sultanas, and I obediently lifted down the jar. After that it was easier. Crumpet fed sultanas to Ziphwort to distract him, chattering away, while I snipped handful after handful of fur and dropped it into the now empty bean sack. The fur didn't mind the hole, and kindly stayed where I put it.

We'd nearly finished when Grandpa Grimstone's voice rang through the house. 'Crumpet? Where are you?'

I froze, but Crumpet gurgled loudly and pushed open the pantry door. When Grandpa Grimstone saw the state of the kitchen, he started back in shock. 'Where is Gertrude? What happened here? And Crumpet, why aren't you working with your pendulum? You'll only learn to slow things down if you practise.'

There was silence.

And then, of course, Grandpa Grimstone pierced me with his glare. 'Martha Grimstone, you are *not* to distract Crumpet from his studies. I'm very disappointed in you.' He plucked Crumpet from the pantry floor. 'Perhaps you could kindly mention to Gertrude that it's lunchtime.' And he swept away, eyeing the disaster zone that was the kitchen one last time on his way out.

As he left, I heard Crumpet call out, 'Fflpt,' and in answer Ziphwort hopped gracefully into his cage. I reached in, fed him a final sultana, and snipped the very last handful of fur from his hind leg.

There was no way I was going to wake Aunt Gertrude to ask her to make lunch. The kitchen had to be dealt with first. So I hastily threw together a plate of cheese-and-pickle sandwiches and delivered them to the apothecary. Then I rolled up my sleeves and set to work on the floury, beany, eggy mess. Yuck.

FRIDAY

I was spying on Grandpa Grimstone through the hole in my bedroom floor. It's the only way to learn the secrets of the apothecary. The bird had fluttered in through the window and was also peering down the hole, prodding my nose with its beak.

Mrs Fife was in the apothecary. She sneezed, and a cloud of flour shot from her nose. She coughed violently. Grandpa Grimstone placed his hand on her shoulder.

'You have Floritis, Mrs Fife,' he said kindly. 'It is a respiratory complaint, common amongst bakery workers. Luckily it's easy to treat, though preparation of the medicinal snortwood cakes takes thirteen days, I'm afraid. Come back in two weeks, and you'll be breathing clearly soon after.'

Snortwood Cake Recipe

CURES FLORITIS AND SEVERAL OTHER RESPIRATORY CONDITIONS.

Grind snortwood flowers with pomegranate syrup in a stone bowl until a thick paste forms. The paste must be the exact consistency of inner-core magma. (Allow several hours.)

Spread paste on papyrus parchment and dry in the sun for thirteen days. In the meteorological event of wind, rain, hail, snow etc, the paste will be ruined, in which case commence procedure again.

After thirteen days, the paste will be hard and brittle. Break into shards and grind back into a powder. Add the sap of the gateaux gateaux tree (commonly known as bonnemilk). Add a pinch of aeratio and form into small cakes. Bake at precisely five hundred and twelve degrees for eight minutes.

Dosage: one cake daily until cured.

Please note: despite snortwood's pleasant cinnamon aroma, the flavour of these cakes is medicinal rather than culinary.

Makes 12 cakes.

Grandpa Grimstone collected our snortwood from a tropical island many years ago. It needs to be kept in a warm, moist environment or it refuses to grow. That's why our snortwood, which grows by the crypt, lives beneath a large bell cloche, and why, every night, August places a fresh hot water bottle inside the dome.

Warm, moist snortwood

I hurried outside to pick the snortwood for Grandpa Grimstone. The bird followed me, chirping melodiously. Grandpa is always asking me to fetch this herb or that one, and I knew he'd be delighted if I delivered what he needed before he even had to ask. See: more proof that I'm responsible, not impetuous.

But down at the crypt, when I asked the spike-berries to move aside so I could see the snortwood, I discovered the bell cloche upturned, and also –

DISASTER – the snortwood nibbled all the way to the ground! Even the bird squawked in horror.

Shortly thereafter, I was distracted by the *most adorable* sight:

Tillipilli has had babies!!!

No snortwood?!

It didn't take a genius to work out what had happened to the snortwood, for Tillipilli snorted aggressively when she saw me, and I smelled the distinct aroma of cinnamon on her breath. Just then I heard Grandpa Grimstone coming down the path. I carefully shifted the bell cloche out of sight beneath a bush and straightened up, looking as innocent as possible.

'There you are, Martha,' Grandpa said. 'I was searching for you, to ask you to pick me some snortwood. But since I'm here, I'll do it myself.' He leaned through the spikeberries, which graciously curled their thorns out of the way, and peered at the ground. Without the bell cloche there as a marker, however, it was tricky to see exactly where the snortwood should have been. Grandpa Grimstone scratched his forehead in confusion. 'I did think the snortwood grew here. Perhaps August has moved it. Do you know where August is, Martha? No? Don't worry, I'll find him myself.' And he wandered off, muttering.

As soon as Grandpa was out of sight I reached beneath the bush again and cradled the bell cloche tenderly in my arms. Tillipilli was still inside, snorting wildly, and her beautiful little babies were still cuddling about her, snuggling into their mama and each other, to keep warm. Oh, they were exquisite! Their skin was wrinkly and too big for their bodies, pink with just a touch of white fluff, like crinkly mice. There were two of them, and—

TWO?? *Weren't there more babies before?*

A movement in the garden caught my eye, and I realised with a start that it was a baby rabbit – it must have escaped the bell cloche while I'd spoken to Grandpa Grimstone. Now it was scuttling off through the herbs, nibbling on the leaves. I glanced around wildly and gasped to see several more baby rabbits hopping about, exploring the garden. How many had there been to begin with? Fifteen? Twenty? I wasn't sure. Oh dear!

I had to catch the escaped babies, but I didn't dare let go of Tillipilli and the other babies until they were safely caged, in case they escaped, too. I sped to the house and put the rabbits gently into the ornate cage with Ziphwort, who squeaked with delight. They looked very crowded in the small cage all together, but of course the castle was no longer safe thanks to the escape route.

By the time I reached the garden again the rest of the babies had vanished. The only sign they'd ever been there were the many nibbled edges to the various herbs' leaves, and a tiny puff of white fur left behind on one of the spikeberry's thorns. Oh dear.

Oh dear, oh dear, oh dear!

FRIDAY

Dear Diary, forgive me for not writing for an entire week, but I've been searching and searching the garden and the house every day for the lost rabbits. I'd imagined I could track them by following a trail of nibbled leaves and snagged white fur – Martha the Magnificent Lady of Astute Detection – but I've found nothing, not a single new clue left behind.

Luckily today I had something interesting to do, which helped distract me a little, temporarily at least. In the name of study, Aunt Gertrude allowed me to spend the morning with Mama, learning to spin. (Meanwhile she popped back to her bed for a quick snooze before lunch.)

In case you've never spun before, I'll show you what to do.

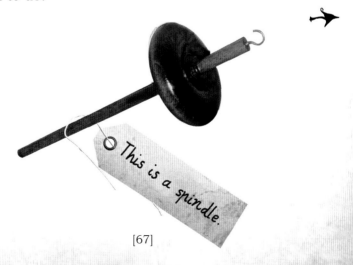

This is a spindle.

SPINNING FOR BEGINNERS
By Mme Denier

STEP 1. Tie a piece of yarn to the spindle, wind the yarn around the spindle and loop it through the hook at the top of the spindle (see A).

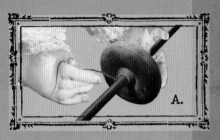

STEP 2. Attach fur to yarn. Suspend the spindle from one hand and spin it in a clockwise direction so the yarn becomes very twisted. While it is spinning, pinch the yarn and a bit of fur with the other hand and stretch out the fur.

STEP 3. Slide the
first hand up over
the stretched-out
fur, so that the
twist rises into this
fur and turns it
into yarn. When
there's no more
stretched fur, pinch
firmly, and with the
other hand, tease
out some more
stretched fur (see C).
Repeat until the
yarn is so long
that the spindle
almost touches the
floor.

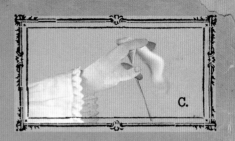

C.

STEP 4: Stop the
spindle from
spinning and wind
on the twisted yarn
(see D). Keep enough
yarn to slip back
through the hook
of the spindle with
a couple of extra
inches to spare. Now
tease out the fluff
at the end and add
in a bit more fur.

D.

Return to STEP 2. Repeat STEPS 2, 3 and 4.

Well, that's what Mama told me, anyway.

The reality is a bit different.

The first time I tried to join Ziphwort's fur to the yarn, the spindle fell to the floor with a sharp

'Mama! It didn't join.'

Mama fed the sleeve of Mr Sterling's new suit into the sewing machine. 'Overlap more,' she said over the whirr.

This time Ziphwort's fur *did* join. Victory! But with an enormous lump. And suddenly, without my having any control, the entire fistful of fur I'd been holding had twisted into a fat rope.

'This won't make a fine fabric like arach-narina,' I complained.

'Mwwmfph,' Mama said, her mouth full of pins.

'What?'

Mama sighed, stopped the machine, and took the pins out of her mouth. 'You'll need to practise making finer thread. You're not ready to start the pure Angora thread for your special fabric yet. Un-twist it, tease it back into fluff, and pull it out into a thin sausage, ready to twist a nice fine thread.'

Ziphwort's fur didn't want to untwist, and I glared at it. I bashed it against the sewing table.

'Martha! You bumped me! I shall have to unpick this seam now and re-sew.'

'Sorry.'

Finally the fur cooperated and I teased it back to a cloud. THIN, THIN, THIN, I told myself, pulling it into an airy, cloudy snake.

At first my next attempt was beautiful. I spun three inches of the loveliest fine thread you've ever seen. And then ·········· *CLANK.*

Oops. It became too fine and broke.

'Mama? How do I rejoin it without a lump?'

Mama took a deep breath and stopped the machine again. 'Untwist the end of the yarn on the spindle, fluff it out as far as you can, and overlap with the new fur.'

'Huh?' But I tried it, and it worked. For a few inches, anyway.

CLANK.

The spindle rolled across the floor and jammed itself under the pedal of Mama's sewing machine.

'Martha! You cannot keep interrupting me like this! If I take too long to sew this suit, Mr Sterling will reject it, as he did last time. I thought Gertrude was supposed to be educating you each morning.'

'This *is* my education, Mama. I'm studying textiles.'

'Perhaps you could study on the other side of the room, and speak a little less while you learn.'

I felt hot, angry tears well up in my eyes.

IT'S NOT FAIR!

Why do Mama and Grandpa Grimstone refuse to teach me their knowledge? Why am I stuck with Aunt Gertrude, who is only interested in imparting the secrets of exponential growth? Why can't Mama *want* to spend just one morning with me, showing me what she knows? I blinked, then darted out my tongue, rescuing my tears from my cheeks and swallowing them before they could *plink* onto Mama's sewing table like little raindrops.

I crawled under the sewing table and rescued my spindle, and then huffed over to the window, as far from Mama as I could get.

I was just about to rejoin the thread when Grandpa Grimstone put his head around the door.

'Martha, are you *sure* you haven't seen that snortwood plant? August swears it was by the crypt.'

I kept my eyes on the spindle and shrugged.

'Martha?'

It was TRUE I hadn't actually *seen* the snortwood – because it had been eaten up. But there's no hiding anything from Grandpa Grimstone. His eyes bored into me like red-hot needles, and the air inside me became so warm and tight that my rescued tears evaporated into steam clouds.

'Oh, all right then,' I burst out a few moments later. 'Tillipilli ate it.' The steam clouds sighed their relief.

Grandpa Grimstone sank his head into his hands and shook it slowly. Finally he straightened up. 'Take my Magnanamator outside and see if Tillipilli dropped any seeds while she was munching. We may be able to germinate a new plant from them. Otherwise I'll have to return to El Haroochimer Island immediately, before Mrs Fife's condition worsens.'

The last time Grandpa Grimstone went on one of his herb-collecting voyages everyone in the village became very grim since there was no one to tend their ailments. I politely suggested Grandpa should teach *me* everything he knows, immediately, so I could fill his shoes while he was away. He just glared at me. I sighed patiently and said, 'In that case, Grandpa Grimstone, perhaps *I* should go to El Haroochimer Island and fetch the new snortwood plant for you.'

Unfortunately this only motivated Grandpa Grimstone to grab his Magnanamator and go and search for the seeds himself, grumping as he went about how I couldn't be trusted with even the smallest task. Clearly he now thinks I'm too impetuous to *ever* leave the village. There is

NO CHANCE he'll let me go to music school now, even if I *do* manage to somehow make amends for Lady Sterling's fabric.

Thankfully Grandpa Grimstone did find some seeds in the crypt garden, and even came to my room as I was writing in you now, Dear Diary, to apologise for having been a bit severe.

Still, I have decided there is no need to mention that Tillipilli was an escapee at the time of her snortwood feast…or the babies.

Place blanket over cage at night to keep baby rabbits warm and feeling safe

MONDAY

All weekend while I practised my spinning (my thread is only a bit lumpy now) I found my mind drifting to the whirlwind. I suppose I can't quite get it out of my head after all.

Something about the whirling of the spindle put me in mind of the whirlwind, and as it spun I found my head whizzing a little, too, until we were in a rhythm: me, the spindle and the imagined whirlwind, all twisted up together and making music of our own, which seemed to be singing:

Stomp on, squish on, flatten the whirlwind...

...over and over again.

Which got me to thinking about how my music *has* to be able to manipulate that whirlwind. Just imagine how grand it would be, Diary, if I *am* right, and if stopping that warning sign – the whirlwind – would actually mean no storm to follow! We'd never have to board up another window again, and all the herbs would bloom so busily we'd be selling them to folk from all over, not just Lady Sterling!

I know how to call a breeze from over yonder, and calm a gale, and coax a freezing finger of air creeping up your back into a buttery-warm caress – but to squish a whirling, seething little tempest of a whirlwind into *nothing*? That isn't how things work.

I could try sending it back to the woods, likc Grandpa Grimstone does with his incantations – but we'd still have to deal with the edge of the storm, and that's nasty enough for our poor little herbs.

I expect I must learn to *calm* a whirlwind…but they are such devilish things, I imagine this would be no easy task – and if the whirlwind still existed, albeit in a calm state, would that really stop the storm from coming along after it? Perhaps the storm would be less wild, and at least that would be something…

If only I could go to the Queen's Music Academy. I *know* someone there could help.

FRIDAY

TING went our champagne-glass doorbell. I tried my new trick: a headstand on the banister at the top of the stairs, followed by a graceful slide down while remaining perfectly upside down, toes to the sky and pointed like a ballerina. It almost worked this time, except for the flip-landing. I hurled myself into the front door with a huge

THUD

I opened it, rubbing my hip.

Mrs Fife stood at the entrance. 'Good morning, Miss Grimst—' She exploded in a fit of coughing, and flour swirled violently around her hair.

'Do come in.' I wondered if Floritis was contagious and stepped right back. 'I'm so sorry, but your snortwood cakes are not ready yet.'

'But Mr Grimstone told me

fourteen days precisely, and here I am,' Mrs Fife cried. 'I've sneezed up enough flour by now to make a generous serve of jam rolls, and I'm *desperate* for my relief.'

'We've had an unforeseen circumstance, I'm afraid,' I said timidly. 'The snortwood plant was unavailable. Grandpa Grimstone found some seeds, and we are germinating them urgently, but I'm afraid it will be a few more weeks at best before you'll have your snortwood cakes.'

For a moment I thought Mrs Fife was going to cry. Her eyes grew red and popped alarmingly. Then she sneezed instead, and I jumped sideways to avoid being embraced by a cloud of flour.

'Toadheads and trollberries,' wailed Mrs Fife, 'all my trials have come at once. Not only is my health giving me grief, but the entire village has gone to shreds.'

I stared at her, perplexed. 'What do you mean, gone to shreds?'

'Those white fluff balls! Haven't you seen them? Good lord, no one knows what they are or where they came from, but they are demolishing everything. My own vegetable garden is nothing but bare soil, and my family was depending on that food. Every cabbage, every carrot, *gone*.'

Alarmed, I shuffled Mrs Fife out the door as quickly as possible. Oh dear, oh dear, OH DEAR. I thought I might know just what the problem was.

I raced to the apothecary and rescued Crumpet from his pendulum-and-hourglass practice. 'Quick! We've an emergency! I think the baby rabbits are eating the town.'

I snuck Crumpet out of the apothecary through the window. The first thing we saw when we landed on the ground outside was a handful of tiny white fluff balls scuttling off behind the house. I realised that the weeds in front of the house were shorter and stubbier than usual, too. It wasn't only the village that was suffering from fluff-ball invasion!

I set Crumpet down and chased after some of the rabbits. My head was ringing with Aunt Gertrude's description of exponential growth. How many baby rabbits had escaped? Thirteen? Eighteen? And would they have had time to grow and make babies of their own yet? I'd read that rabbits reproduce awfully quickly. I did some maths (I'm quicker than Aunt Gertrude thinks):

➤

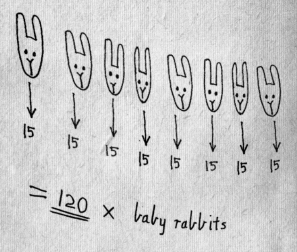

15   15   15   15   15   15   15   15

$= \underline{\underline{120}} \times$ baby rabbits

Say eight of the babies were girls. And each of those girls had, what, say fifteen babies. Well, there could be one hundred and twenty brand-new rabbits at large. Or more. And if we didn't round up those bunnies, within weeks there would be even more: over a thousand rabbits!

Time was of the essence.

I dived onto my belly after a fluff ball. It hopped neatly out of reach.

Crumpet was having better luck; his three legs make him quick. By the time I turned around he was holding two of the cutest little rabbits I had ever seen. When I'd first seen Tillipilli's babies they'd been pink and mouse-like, but these rabbits had grown into round puffs of white fur, and if you looked carefully you could just see a pair of ears in there. We took them to the house and added them to the ornate rabbit cage from the pedlar.

I gave Ziphwort a pat and rubbed his ears; then I stroked Tillipilli's little fluffy face. They stared up at me imploringly, as if to say, 'Can we come out?'

But I shook my head. 'Soon,' I promised them.

Just then August emerged from his bedroom, his hair squashed flat on one side, sticking straight up on the other. 'Goodness, is it midday already, Miss Martha?'

'It's well past noon. Now you're up, August, will you tie Crumpet to my back? We've got to get to town – urgently.'

'Of course.' He rubbed his eyes and stared, bewildered, at the rabbit cage – he'd spotted the babies. 'They'll be needing more room, I think.'

I nodded, sighing deeply. 'But the castle has an escape tunnel dug through it. We can't put the rabbits in there.'

'Just let me have a cup of tea, and I'll put down a wooden floor for you. Then they won't be able to dig their way out.'

I smiled at August gratefully. With Crumpet on my back, I hurried quick as I could down the path to the village, stumbling in my haste, the bird fluttering behind me, pecking at my plaits to hurry me along. It wasn't easy since only one of my boots was properly laced; I still hadn't gotten around to fixing the other one, which Ziphwort had nibbled on when he'd first arrived.

I stopped short when I arrived at Thredneedle Road. Mrs Fife had been right: there were fluff balls *everywhere*, and the village was in utter chaos.

Right in the middle of the road, a wagon had collapsed into a hole. I stared in confusion. A rabbit had done *that*?

As if reading my mind, Frankie Emmerson slid up beside me. 'Those fluff balls have burrowed a huge network of tunnels right under the town, and now the road caves in if anything heavy drives over it. Have you any idea what they are?'

I had every idea, but there was no way I was admitting it to Frankie. He's my only friend. He lives on the dairy farm at the bottom of the hill, on the very edge of the village. I couldn't risk him finding out that I was entirely responsible for this disaster.

'Look.' Frankie pointed to the water tank next to the blacksmith's. There was a rabbit-toothed bite out of its base and the water was draining out in a steady trickle, flooding the road and turning it to mud. 'And they've ruined our hay. All the bales we had stacked for winter have been spread across the field. Papa is hopping mad.'

'I'm going to round them up,' I declared.

Frankie tilted his freckled face and squinted at me. 'We've all been trying for days. None of us has managed to catch a single one. Not one. So we don't know what they are, or what to do.'

As we walked down Thredneedle Road, my boots squished tiny pellets of rabbit poop into the ground. They dotted the village, rolling off porches and tumbling from the roofs of the cottages. I wondered if a village could eventually *drown* in rabbit poop.

Mr Sterling's grain sacks were stacked by his front door, and I saw that every single sack had a bite-hole in it. But the irony was, the rabbits hadn't *eaten* the grain – it was spread across the garden, soggy in the mud. They had dined on Mr Sterling's snapdragons instead.

It wasn't until I arrived at Mrs Golding's, however, that the enormity of the problem truly hit me. I gasped. Mrs Golding grows magnificent roses: giant blooms with petals the size of watermelons. Every year travellers from far beyond our valley visit to admire them, and to purchase cuttings at great expense. Mrs Golding's roses were now just bare, thorny stalks.

'Crumpet,' I hissed, 'we are going to need your magic to deal with this. Have you by any chance learned an … uh … *antithesis for exponential growth* spell?'

'*Umphh*,' said Crumpet.

Of course! He'd been learning about how to slow things down using his magic. If we could just find him a pendulum, I thought, he'd be able to slow the rabbits, and then we could catch them.

'Quick!' I ordered Frankie. 'Fetch Crumpet the pendulum from the church clock!'

Frankie's eyes widened in alarm, and his curly red hair stood straight up. 'I couldn't do that! The vicar would have me for dinner.'

I always have to do *everything* myself.

Once I'd shimmied up the tower, removed the pendulum using my small pocket-spanner and handed it to Crumpet, I dusted myself off and stared at him expectantly.

Crumpet held the pendulum towards the fluff balls on Mrs Golding's porch. He waved it mysteriously, his brows furrowed in concentration. But nothing happened. The rabbits bounded through the stubs of the garden, dived under the fence, and hopped down the road, as fast as ever.

'*Brmmp*,' Crumpet declared, dejected.

He couldn't do it. He hadn't practised enough!

Devilsnake eyeballs. I stomped my foot, and my

unlaced boot slipped right off. I tugged it back on and glared at Frankie. 'Okay then, we're going to need carrots and fishing nets. Surely you can help me gather some basic supplies?'

Frankie trotted off obediently, and I pulled the lace out of my other boot. While we waited for his return, Crumpet and I set to work:

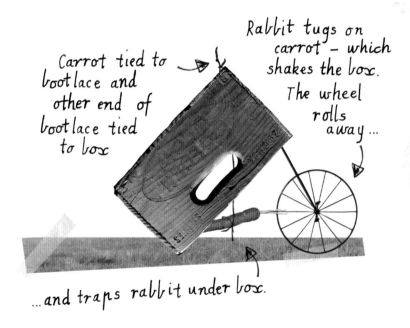

Carrot tied to bootlace and other end of bootlace tied to box

Rabbit tugs on carrot – which shakes the box. The wheel rolls away ...

...and traps rabbit under box.

At first our trap worked just perfectly. We put Frankie's carrot in the middle and stood back. The first rabbit hopped straight in after it, and was imprisoned by the box.

"HOORAY!"

I shouted, jumping up too fast and tripping on my loose boot, tangling my ankles. *Ouch*. I kicked the boots off, still jubilant. 'We need to make lots of traps, LOTS of them. Frankie, more carrots!'

I retrieved the imprisoned rabbit and trapped it in the fishing net.

We added a second rabbit, and a third. Brilliant! In a few hours we'd have them all!

But just as I was setting the fourth trap, the first rabbit chewed a hole through the net ... and they all scampered off.

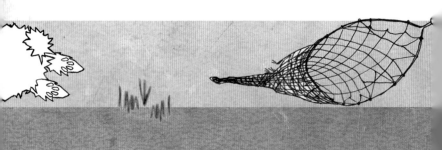

Crumpet, Frankie and I stared in dismay.

I sighed. 'Crumpet, we're going home. We'll have to look up a spell for this.'

Grandpa Grimstone was in the garden bent over the tray of snortwood seedlings when I trudged heavily through the front gate carrying my boots, Crumpet on my back. At Grandpa's feet sat a perfect circle of white fluff balls. I froze, and was having make-me-invisible thoughts when Grandpa Grimstone straightened up and pierced me with his sharp eyes.

'Martha Grimstone, did you fail to mention to me that your rabbits had reproduced?'

'Uhmm.' I stared at the ground.

'Did you allow them to escape?'

I stared at the ground some more.

'Do you know what you have done, Martha? Not only have you endangered Mrs Fife's life through your destruction of the snortwood plant, but now you have endangered our entire valley! Any moment now, those rabbits will arrive in the village and wreak havoc. We must contain them before that happens.'

I gulped, and closed my mouth as firmly as I could. So he didn't know…

But on my back, Crumpet said, 'Urgghp.' Which meant: *Too late.*

Grandpa's eyes widened. He sprang to action. 'Crumpet, to the apothecary! We must deal with this immediately.' He lifted Crumpet from my back.

'But Grandpa, it wasn't ME who destroyed the snortwood, or the village—'

'You cared for those rabbits in an irresponsible manner, Martha Grimstone. I'm sure you'll understand now why I consider you too impetuous to leave home. How could we possibly expect Lady Sterling to clean up after all your disasters?'

And with that, Grandpa Grimstone swept away, taking Crumpet with him, leaving me standing barefoot by the gate feeling very, very small.

As I stood there rescuing the tears that flowed down my cheeks, my hurt slowly turned to anger.

It had been my idea to go to the apothecary and search for magical solutions. Once again, I was SHUT OUT from everything good and interesting and exciting that happened around here. And everything BAD that happened — well, somehow it was always MY FAULT.

I ought to run away, I thought. No, I WILL run away! The only place I knew of to run to was Lady Sterling's, though, and she wouldn't have me. I knew that. I'd end up sleeping in a ditch somewhere.

Oh, what was the use of ANYTHING?

A ditch it would have to be !!!

When I charged into the house to pack, though, somehow I found myself upstairs instead, standing before the Epithium.

AND SUDDENLY I HAD IT.

The whirlwind was like Mama's yarn. I didn't need to squash it, or shift it, or calm it – I needed to *uncoil it*, the way I'd unthreaded my yarn. Uncoil and fluff out each strand, eliminating their collective strength. But to unthread yarn, first you had to understand how to spin it in the first place.

I had to learn to coil a whirlwind with my music – and then later I could learn the song's inverse, and play the music inside out to uncoil and disperse the impish little devil into a mere thread of ordinary, harmless wind!

I dropped my boots, wiped my hands on my dress, and sank down onto the plush, velvet seat of the Epithium. My eyes burning, my chest still swollen with anger, I struck the strings harshly with my fingers. The notes jarred, discordant and brassy, bouncing off the walls and bruising me with their temper. As I played, a channel opened inside of me, and all my hurt and frustration flowed out – out through my arms and my fingers, exploding around me in a tumultuous uproar.

That's when I saw it. The curtain billowed towards me, although there was no breeze. I sobbed and played harder, more fiercely, as though my entire being were on fire. The rug on the floor lifted its corner and rolled towards me. The books on the shelf slid off and circled me, spiralling inwards, as though I were the eye of a whirlwind. Abruptly, I took my fingers from the strings, and in the sudden silence the curtain sagged and the books fell to the floor. I played again and they rose, coiling towards me.

Inspiration struck again! I still hadn't the faintest idea how to turn a melody inside out – but I *did* know, now, how to solve our most immediate problem:

THE RABBITS.

I raced through the house calling for August but couldn't find him anywhere. He'd nailed down the promised wooden flooring to the rabbit castle, but he wasn't there either. Finally I spied him coming down through the woods behind the house, Aunt Gertrude's arm threaded through his. I hurtled towards them, breathing hard, trying to catch my breath. Aunt Gertrude mistook my urgency for a scolding, and said defensively, 'Due to our reprehensible working hours, Martha, we have decided to take our strolls in the afternoon. It's a little uncustomary, I grant you.'

'Good idea,' I panted. 'August, will you help me bring the Epithium down to the rabbit cage, *right now*? Please?'

'Of course, Miss Martha.' He extricated himself from Aunt Gertrude, and a little later, just as dusk was falling, the Epithium stood grandly in the middle of the rabbit castle, Tillipilli and Ziphwort crouching beside it, their babies scampering around to explore.

I sat astride its seat and began to play. At first I achieved nothing, just an empty melody. Ziphwort leapt onto my lap and curled up there, encouragement in his eyes. Tillipilli stretched out at my feet, her paws resting lightly on my toes.

I breathed deeply, trying to conjure back my anger – the fire that had set my music alive. I remembered the Queen's Music Academy; Mama scolding me; and Grandpa Grimstone's back as he strode away to share his magical talents with Crumpet alone. My blood began to **boil**, and so did the notes. Soon the whole valley was seething, tree branches crackling, leaves straining towards me, loose bark and grit coiling inwards towards the castle. The notes screeched and thundered, and if my hands hadn't been busy I'd have shoved my fingers into my ears to shut out the sound.

Instead I shifted my focus to the rabbits, calling them, rather than the wind, with my notes – reaching far and wide to catch each one in a tangle of melody and lure it towards me. Despite the cacophony, they started to come: a long, slow line of fluff balls, sucked into the inferno of my music. They spiralled up the hill, coiled around the house, and blew in through the double doors of the castle, landing delicately at my feet. *It worked!*

Then the people came: Mama, Grandpa Grimstone, Crumpet and Aunt Gertrude. Drawn by my crashing, rolling refrain, they surrounded the castle, and I looked up to find all eyes on me. The last rabbit blustered in, and August closed the door. With a final strum, I lowered my hands and the music died away into silence.

For a long time no one said anything. Then Mama breathed, 'Martha, you've such magick in your hands, such talent. We cannot waste your gift.'

Mama stared meaningfully at Grandpa Grimstone. There was more silence.

At last, Grandpa Grimstone said, 'Velvetta speaks the truth, Martha. Such talent does need to be trained – controlled – or it could become a danger to you. I see so much of your father in you, my dear. What are we to do with you? It's evident you're too young to leave home.'

'But time is of the essence,' Mama said. 'It's important to start young. I'm sure Lady Sterling could keep a firm rein on her.'

Grandpa Grimstone sighed. 'Perhaps...'

My heart burst in little sparkly fire-pops of exhilaration. Then there was *hope* for the Queen's Music Academy? *HOPE* for learning how to inverse my whirlwind music?

But I didn't dare to jump for joy quite yet, for I had a feeling that once Lady Sterling found out what I'd done to her fabric, she'd declare me unfit for boarding in her stately home.

'I'm sure I could learn to look after Crumpet, so that Martha is free to go.' Mama smiled at me.

'And I could do Martha's daily chores,' August offered.

Aunt Gertrude frowned. 'Excuse me, I think we may be getting ahead of ourselves here. What are we going to do with *these*?' She gestured to the rabbits. 'They must be banished.'

'Noooooo!' I wailed. 'They're far too sweet! They can live right here. August has made them a nice secure floor. And I can use their fur to make a new piece of fabric for Lady Sterling.'

'Martha, do you recall our lessons on exponential growth? It's unworkable. They must go.'

'But not Tillipilli and Ziphwort.'

'They would need to be kept apart. So they couldn't … ahem … *reproduce* further.'

'I can build them separate chambers within the castle,' August offered, 'with a thin wire wall so they will feel like they're together and can even cuddle.'

'Perhaps we could keep the little ones for just a few weeks, for Martha to make the fabric?' Mama suggested.

'Very well. But for two weeks only. Lady Sterling is due to visit in three, so that allows a week for you to sew the dress, Velvetta. Martha, I shall suspend your other lessons so that you may use the time to create the fabric, and learn to weave.'

'Two weeks is not long to make such a fine fabric, Martha,' Mama warned. 'You'll have to work very hard.'

'I will! I'll spin and weave day and night, I promise.'

'Then should the fabric be completed in time,' Grandpa Grimstone declared, 'and should Lady Sterling still be prepared to board you, you may attend the Queen's Music Academy.'

I leapt from the Epithium and rushed to throw my arms around Grandpa Grimstone. But he was bent over, looking closely at what appeared to be a pellet of rabbit poop. Tillipilli's poop, if I wasn't mistaken, for it had a hint of that cinnamon scent and a slight sparkle to it. Grandpa pulled his Magnanamator out of his pocket and squinted at the pellet. Then he let out a mighty, most un-Grandpa-like whoop. 'This is a snortwood cake!' He held it up jubilantly. 'I have never seen such a thing in all my days! Somehow that rabbit has processed the snortwood she ate in exactly the manner needed for the cakes. No need for a thirteen-day wait or the use of expensive papyrus. Quick! Fetch Mrs Fife! We'll have her cured in no time.'

'May I suggest,' said Aunt Gertrude, 'that you abstain from fetching Mrs Fife until the *cakes* are packaged in a manner that no longer resembles excrement? She might be more amenable to taking her medicine if it was presented in a more palatable form.'

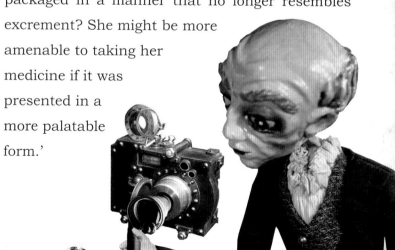

THURSDAY

I've done it! I've worked out how to weave! See my
loom:

resting nest
for bird

Designed and
built by Martha
Grimstone

spoon
one

spoon
two

Quails hold
threads
tight

To operate Quailoom:

1. Collect quails from quail house and summon bird.
2. Feed bird and quails to ensure they have energy.
3. Give end of Angora yarn to bird to hold firmly in her beak.
4. Lift spoon one to raise half of the threads on the loom.
5. Bird flies through the gap made by the lifted and not-lifted threads (bird must fly from left to right).
6. Lower spoon one and lift spoon two.
7. Bird passes through gap in threads again (from right to left).
8. Lower spoon two.
9. Repeat steps #4 to #8 until woven fabric is desired length.
10. Feed bird and quails again, and return quails to quail house.

Thank goodness for the quails. And for Crumpet, who sits beside me orchestrating them: 'Phnn. Chypff. Dooooopff.'

We were all crowded into Mama's sewing room from dawn again this morning, hard at work on the new fabric for Lady Sterling – me, Mama, Crumpet, the quails and my bird.

'Mama, you should have done this years ago,' I said. 'Then you could have spun and woven your very own fabrics. You didn't need your grandmother to teach you.'

The quails wove the last threads into the fabric for the sleeve, and fluttered it over to Mama's sewing table. She took it immediately and began stitching it to the bodice. The instant any piece is ready, Mama adds it to the gown. So far there's a bodice front, a bodice back and one sleeve. But the biggest piece of fabric is yet to come: the skirt, which will need yards and yards of *angorina*. See, I've named my fabric, since it can't really be called arachnarina. One day it'll be highlighted at the front of Bobbin & Co's catalogue, fetching a very high price, I'm sure.

'Martha, when one's grandmother vanishes, one doesn't tend to feel very inventive. And in any case, my family never had quails when I was a girl. Perhaps I was just waiting for *you*.'

 **CLANK.** My spindle hit the floor.

The bird flew down from her perch on the loom and nudged it with her beak, rolling it towards me.

I try to spin fast enough to keep up with the quails, which takes considerable concentration, but every now and then the entire flock has to stop work while I rejoin and catch up. My thread isn't perfectly smooth, unlike the thread Mama spun when she demonstrated for me. But strangely enough, once woven into the fabric, the little bumps even out, and there's just a hint of lacy texture as a result. It's beautiful, my **angorina** – fine, light, warm and exquisitely soft.

'Yes, I think I *was* waiting for you, Martha. It is a treat to have you sitting there realising the dream I've had since I was a little girl. And I do enjoy our chats. To think one day soon you could be at the Queen's Music Academy, far away.' Mama sighed sadly.

'Oh, Mama, you needn't worry yet. Once Lady Sterling finds out what I did to her arachnarina, there's no hope she'll let me board with her. *I* think the *angorina* is lovely, but she mightn't agree, and I expect she'll be very angry with me.'

Mama threaded the needle on her machine and smiled at me fondly. 'I think it's you who needn't worry, Martha.'

But I can't help it. I worry day and night, because I simply *must* go to the Queen's Music Academy, I *must*. The valley needs me, the whirlwinds need dispersing, and I've still no idea how to play the inverse of my new melody. There are only two weeks until Lady Sterling's visit, and every time I think of it my skin grows hot, my heart pounds with a hundred little hammers, and I become so choked in my chest I can scarcely breathe.

SATURDAY

I'm sorry for neglecting you, Dear Diary. I thought I would never get Lady Sterling's skirt completed. But last night I wove the final threads of the skirt, and Mama stitched it straight to the gown, which is now wrapped and ready, awaiting Lady Sterling's visit tomorrow. The weaving took a whole week longer than it was supposed to, but thanks to Mama's technique of sewing each piece as it was created we didn't run out of time. Phew.

This morning was the market. It was in a village on the other side of our valley, but happily Mr Johnson agreed to take August and me in his cart. The rabbits travelled in the back, in a trunk I'd found in the attic. The market was much bigger than the one on our green. The stink was intoxicating, and I had to fight to mind my manners and not hold my dress against my nose. August carried the trunk to the animal barn, and we stood against the wall surrounded by sheep, pigs, goats and poultry.

'August, would you excuse me a moment? Don't sell any of the rabbits yet, please. I just need to do something.'

'Certainly, Miss Martha.' August closed the lid of the trunk and sat on it. 'You do as you need. But you mustn't be long, as we need time to sell the rabbits and for me to buy the supplies before Mr Johnson heads home.'

I ran fast, dodging the crowd, scanning the stalls and barrows piled high with goods. I'd almost covered the entire market and was about to turn back to the barn when I finally saw what I'd been looking for. The pedlar!

He stood beside his gypsy wagon, straightening a row of ribbons and laces. The silver ring sat in the same place I'd last seen it, the ruby glistening intoxicatingly.

'Hello,' I said shyly.

He peered down at me. 'What are you wanting, girl? Some pretty ribbons?'

'Do you remember me?' I asked.

He stared at me properly then, and his face lit up. 'Of course! You're the memsparkym girl! I can't tell you how thrilled the Pommingtons were with their cure. Mrs Pommington is right as rain, and Alfred's so grateful that he and the boys can get back to their usual jobs. Only trouble is they used to make their living from rabbits, but they gave them all away.'

'I know,' I said. 'I bought them. Well, two of them, anyway.'

The pedlar squinted at me. 'That's right, so you did. Don't suppose you'd be wanting to sell them back?'

I shook my head. 'Not those two. But they had

babies. I can sell you the babies if you like. Remember how you said one rabbit was worth one memsparkym flower, and that ring over there was worth a hundred memsparkym flowers? Does this mean the ring is worth a hundred rabbits?'

'Errr. Well. I guess so.'

'I have a hundred baby rabbits! I'll trade you the ring for the babies?'

The pedlar scratched his head. 'I'm not sure the Pommingtons will be wanting a hundred rabbits…'

'But they could buy however many they want, and you'd have more left over to sell.'

'Hmm. Why not? All right, girl – where are the rabbits?'

'You wait. I'll get August to bring you the trunk. And don't sell the ring before we get here.'

SUNDAY

I didn't need to wait for the *TING* of the champagne glass, for I was watching from the landing window as Lady Sterling glided through the gate. I opened the door and there she stood, wearing an elegant gown of crimson silk layered with delicate lace. Her white hair was arranged ornately on top of her head. She looked like a queen.

I curtseyed, even though I'm not usually one to do so. 'Do come in, Lady Sterling.' At the sound of my voice, Aunt Gertrude hurried from the kitchen, Grandpa Grimstone appeared from the apothecary with Crumpet on his hip, and Mama floated down the stairs carrying the packages containing Lady Sterling's new gown and Mr Sterling's new suit.

Lady Sterling allowed Grandpa Grimstone to kiss her hand and embraced Mama and Aunt Gertrude, kissing them both on each cheek. Then she took my face between her hands. 'Martha, I can't tell you how delighted I am to see you.'

I gave a small, nervous smile, knowing that once she found out about the burnt arachnarina her delight would turn to dismay.

Aunt Gertrude took Lady Sterling's cloak and ushered us into the parlour. As she offered up a tray of pastries and fruit, Lady Sterling took hold of her hand. 'What a charming ring! I'm sure you didn't have this when I last visited?'

Aunt Gertrude blushed and nodded. 'August and I announced our engagement just yesterday. He proposed to me on our walk.'

'He's a lucky man, your August. I do wish my son would make such a fine match. I'd had hopes Furchell might ask for your hand in marriage, but I see we have moved too slowly.'

Lady Sterling took a pastry and turned to me. 'Martha, I do hope you've thought about my invitation to attend the Queen's Music Academy and board with me. They are terribly excited to meet you after all I've told them.'

I took a deep breath. 'Lady Sterling, I have a confession to make.' I flushed a deep crimson. 'I, err ... something happened to the fabric you sent us. Uhm ... an unforeseen circumstance. And, I, err ... may have ruined it. But I've made you a new fabric. And Mama sewed your gown from that. And I do hope it's all right – that you'll still accept it.'

'Goodness, Martha,' she said, bemused, 'perhaps I'd better see it for myself.'

Mama handed her the parcel. Lady Sterling unwrapped it and drew in her breath sharply. At first I thought she was angry, but then I realised it was awe. 'Martha Grimstone, did you say you *made* this material? This is glorious! What is it? Don't tell me you keep spiders under the house?'

'No, ma'am. It's made from Angora.'

'She spun every thread herself, and wove it into this lovely fabric,' Mama said, wrapping her arm around my shoulder proudly.

'Well, the quails helped. And Crumpet.'

Lady Sterling shook out the dress and held it against her shoulders. The long skirt rippled to the floor, understated and elegant, the delicate lacy texture glimmering in the light.

'Velvetta, you are unsurpassed as a seamstress. And one could only use such a restrained design with a spectacular fabric. Even the arachnarina wouldn't have carried this off. Oh, it's a masterpiece! Martha, I'm so glad for your mishap, for this dress will win me the title of style queen of the year.'

'So...' I reddened again, '...you would still have me board with you?'

Lady Sterling laughed heartily and clapped her hands. 'Of course, my dear! Of course!'

A huge bubble of joy swelled from my heart, sprouting enormous, white, feathery wings that fluttered in excitement.

I'M GOING!

I'M REALLY GOING!

I flung my arms around Lady Sterling.

I shall go to the Queen's Music Academy and learn all I need to know about how to use my own special talent, and when I come home again – well, *watch out, whirlwinds*, for I shall soon be sending you on your way! I shall learn control, technique, inversion, inflection, uncoiling, inside-out-ness ... my Dear Diary, I cannot **wait** to get started.

Lady Sterling pulled me in close, and she, Mama, Aunt Gertrude, Crumpet and Grandpa Grimstone smiled fondly at me. At that moment, my world felt the most magnificent it had ever been.

The End

The Making of the Grimstones

Dear Reader,

I made the family of Grimstone puppets myself, and furnished their miniature home. This was for my gothic theatre show, *The Grimstones*. It took me eighteen months to handcraft everything, mostly from recycled junk. They were some of the happiest days of my life, because nothing gives me more pleasure than making things with my own hands.

Since my partner, Paula Dowse, and I began performing with the Grimstones, as puppeteers and narrators for the show, we have toured Australia and the world. It seems that, like me, our audiences have fallen in love with my little puppet family.

Between shows, Martha Grimstone sits on her tiny bed and scrawls in her notebook, unleashing all the

excitements and frustrations of her everyday life. Her words are captivating, her little drawings so enchanting, that I can't help myself from sharing them with you. Every time I take one of her notebooks I leave an empty one in its place, and she winks at me, because Martha longs to be famous and can't wait for you to read her diary!

If you would like to know more about the Grimstones, please visit **www.thegrimstones.com**. You can watch them come to life on YouTube, download beautiful photos of their miniature world, and see where they'll be performing next. Find the Grimstones on Facebook, follow them on Twitter, and read my blog.

Online, you can also order *The Grimstones – An Artist's Journal*, which records my creative process while making the Grimstones puppets and show, from my initial spark of an idea through to a theatrical production that has toured the world. It's jam-packed with sketches, beautiful photographs and 'how to' tips, providing inspiration to create and bring more creativity into your life.

Thank you for sharing the Grimstones with me.

Love and creative fire to you!

THE GRIMSTONES

HATCHED

My first diary—lots of secrets inside!
All about Crumpet !!

MORTIMER REVEALED

My second diary—
discover the secrets of
Mortimer's
crypt!

Make sure you read the
first two books in
The Grimstones series
– and watch out for more
from Martha Grimstone!